I0626384

ONE THING
ABOUT
LIFE

LERON ANTHONY STEWART

ONE THING ABOUT LIFE

Copyright © 2020 by Perfect Pen Publishing

CHAPTER 1

I've known Bo since we were in kindergarten. It's a little weird, but we couldn't possibly be more different. I've always been the outspoken one while he lets people walk all over him. He's too damn nice. I've always had to fight his battles. To be honest, I don't even know if Bo knows how to fight. Shit, he never had to!

Bo comes from a complete household. His parents have been married for like a hundred years. Seeing how stable his family is makes me enjoy stopping by his crib. They give him anything he wants. That boy was driving a Benz to school when he was sixteen! Now me, I've always had to do everything on my own. I mean work a nine to five, sell drugs, cut grass, screw cougars…hey, don't judge me. Cougars pay well for young meat. But me driving a Benz to high school? Shiidddd, that wasn't even realistic.

And we were *very* different when it came to the ladies. He probably got his dick wet a few times, but has always been focused on obtaining what his parents have. And who can blame him? I'd look forward to that, too, if that's how I was raised to live. But that's simply not the case with me. I lost my virginity at the age of twelve, and I've been smashing everything ever since. I've run through sisters, cousins, best friends, co-workers and enemies. I haven't made it to mother and daughter yet, but I'm working on it.

We do have one thing in common if nothing else. Sports. I was our high school basketball star while he was our football start. My attitude pretty much cost me a free ride to college, and he got a scholarship to LSU. LSU! He's almost certain to make it to the NFL in a few years. I ended up enrolling in Southern University, so I can be only a few minutes away from Bo. And, oh yeah, so I can party and smash chicks!

Bo

I swear that I couldn't be any more different from my best friend, Dap. Maybe I let people get away with too much at times, but I feel like foolishness is never worth entertaining, so I just let it go. My parents taught me to kill people with kindness. It's been working so far. That fool, Dap, is a hothead though. I can't even tell you how many people he has knocked out. This one guy pulled out a pistol on him, and he walked up to the dude and kissed the barrel of the gun. Said it was a "pretty little pop pistol," and then he just walked off like nothing happened. Now is that crazy or what? It's really weird because he's so cool and peaceful. But once he feels threatened or disrespected, he becomes a different person. And I'm not talking about screaming and making a scene like a lot of fake gangsters do. Most of the time they don't even see it coming, and when it's over he never seems upset or rattled. Talking about one throwed off individual!

A lot of times I wonder if his childhood has an effect on him now. I've never seen his dad before. As a matter of fact, I'm not even sure HE'S seen his dad before. He never talks about him, and I'm afraid to ask him about it. He grew up in the projects, and I think his mom is on welfare. If she ever had a job, I don't know about it, but that's something else that he never talks about. When we were kids, he always came and stayed by our house. My parents love that dude. He would stay for days at a time, sometimes weeks. It was different for him. My parents aren't rich by any means, but they've had their jobs and each other for as long as I can remember. My dad has been at the steel plant for thirty years and is currently a supervisor. My mom is a nurse who absolutely refused to be a stay-at-home mother who depended on my dad for everything. I don't have any brothers and sisters, so they've always spoiled me. That's probably why that clown always feels the need to fight for me all of the time.

We are completely opposite when it comes to women. He probably lost his virginity when he was nine or ten years old; I don't even wanna think about how many chicks he's smashed because I get nervous that he might have caught something that he can't get rid of. I didn't have sex until my senior prom. My girl and I had been dating since tenth grade, and prom night was the first time for both of us. I must admit that I cheated on my girl a few times after we graduated, and I always felt guilty. After the last time, I promised myself that I would never cheat on her again, but she found out about everything and left me. I still love her dearly and I hope that she forgives me and marries me one day. If not…it is what it is.

Dap and I were always good in sports. I knew I was good, but I never thought I was good enough to be playing cornerback for LSU. It's a known fact that if you play for the Tigers, you most likely will be playing on Sundays one day. I'm just going to remain humble and focus on keeping my grade point average up. Now Dap is a natural in basketball. If he would have been dedicated and didn't have such a bad attitude, he would be playing at a Division I school.

He turned down several scholarships to junior colleges just to enroll at Southern to be close to me. It's good to have a friend so loyal, but I think that dude needs therapy.

CHAPTER 2

———

"Whassup, Tiger? Them white girls over there in Tigerland ain't start raping your scary ass yet?"

Bo didn't even have to turn around to know whose voice it was. In fact, he was surprised that Dap went two weeks without harassing him. He finally turned around and greeted his friend in the same manner.

"Whassup, Jaguar? Them sisters over there on the yard ain't burn the head off your dick yet?"

They both broke out in laughter, but Dap couldn't wait to give his ace an update on his brand new college experience. "Nigga, I'm nationwide now! I smashed one from Mobile, one from Detroit, one from L.A., and a couple of 'em from da N.O. They gon know Dap in every state before it's all over!" All Bo could do was shake his head.

Please tell me you're using rubbers on all of these chicks." Before Dap could answer, the front door to Bo's parents' house opened. "Well, hello, my two college boys!" Mrs. Johnson cooked every single Sunday and told the guys that she expected to see them today.

"Hi, Mrs. Johnson. I was just tellin' yo' ugly son that we better get in the house before you come out here and beat us with a tree branch." All Mrs. Johnson could do was laugh. Dap always knew how to keep her smiling, even if she was having a bad day. "Boy, y'all better get in here and wash y'all hands. The food is almost ready."

Bo was still thinking about his last statement to Dap. He answered his mom as he gave his friend a serious stare. "We're about to come in, Mama. I just need to grab a few things out of the car." Mrs. Johnson nodded and went back inside.

"Mannnn, you know how much *more* pussy I'd be getting if I had a Benz?" Dap knew he was getting on Bo's nerves, but he couldn't help himself. "Just lemme use it for a weekend. I wouldn't even get a hotel room. I'd bend 'em right over the back seat!"

Bo couldn't ignore him any longer. "And my whip would probably smell like badussy when I get it back!" Dap couldn't even stand up. He was laughing so hard that he had to take a seat on the curb. Bo shook his head, grabbed his bags, and went inside, leaving his friend alone and laughing.

Just as Dap was getting ready to get up and go inside his phone rang. He didn't even recognize the number but decided to answer anyway.

"Whattup." He usually didn't answer unfamiliar numbers, but he'd given his number to so many females at school that he'd lost count. His mind drifted for a moment as he tried to guess who was giving him a call for the first time. But he was in for a rude awakening....

"I'm pregnant, Daron, and I'm not getting an abortion." The voice sounded familiar, but he still wasn't sure who it was. Dap bit down on his lip in an attempt not to overreact. He took a deep breath and finally responded. "Who is this?"

He most certainly struck a nerve. "What the fuck do you mean 'who is this?' You know who the fuck this is! Daron, don't play games with me!"

"Girl, look, don't come at me with that bullshit. How long has it been? Two? Three months? I know for a fact that you were sleeping with other dudes around the same time I hit. You think you're the only one with kinfolk in Gonzales and Convent? Half of my family done beat that cat up, so get a life and lose my number." He hung up the phone without giving her a chance to respond. As he took a few seconds to pull himself together, the sudden aroma of seafood gumbo hit his nostrils. And just that quickly, the disturbing phone call was forgotten. He stood up and dusted himself off. "I'm about to dive into that pot like it stole something from me. That gumbo won't owe me nothing!"

CHAPTER 3

"Man, I'm full as a tick! I'm ready to get my drink on nah. Let's go shoot pool at the daiquiri shop." Dap knows that he's going to be drinking alone though. Bo doesn't drink. But although everyone knows Dap is not twenty-one, Dap can go into any club or store in Baton Rouge and buy as much alcohol as he likes. Some clubs don't even make him pay for it. They simply allow him to drink on the house all night. Some folks say it's because of how he protects Bo, and everybody loves Bo. Others say it's because people are afraid of Dap. Word on the street has it that he robbed some drug dealers at gunpoint with no mask and killed one guy who took too long to give up his stash. Either way, he's respected and feared just as much as Bo is loved.

"Okay, bruh. We can go for a lil bit, but I can't stay out too late." No argument came from Dap, so they jumped in the Benz and rolled out to their favorite spot.

"Dap and Bo. My main men. What's good, fellas?" Geno, the owner and manager of the local daiquiri shop always gave them a warm greeting. "How's college life treating you two?" The two friends absolutely love Geno. They are the only two under twenty-one that he ever allowed in his spot.

"Everything's good, brother. You know me. If there're women around, I'm Gucci!" Geno and Dap laugh as they shake hands. Bo keeps a straight face as he walks to Geno. " Life's good man. I'm blessed. Just trying to get adjusted to the college level and stay healthy. Probably gonna have to stand out on special teams before I see a lot of time at corner, but I ain't about to wait till my junior or senior season. They gon learn about Lebeau Johnson real soon."

Dap taps Geno on the shoulder. "Ay, that nigga mean that shit. The boy is a maniac. I can't even work out with that fool. I feel sorry for whatever wide receiver that lines up across from him and for whatever running back carries the ball toward his side of the field. He's good enough to be in the league today!" Geno looks at Bo for a second. "I don't doubt it. Not one bit."

Just as Bo was getting ready to grab a pool stick, he remembered some news he had for Dap. "Oh, Dap. I forgot to tell you. Ya boy is coming home in a few days." Tat was Dap's other right hand man before he went to juvie. They did all kinds of wild stuff together in their early teens, but Tat got caught up in a bad situation and ended up with juvenile life for accessory to murder. He'd been gone for four years.

Dap was ecstatic to hear the news. "Are you serious? Last time I asked his mama she said he had a couple years left. I gotta throw him a party. A *real* party. Not a whack ass party. Shiiiiiiiddd, it's going down!"

A barmaid brought Dap his favorite drink and Bo a water without them asking for it. Bo racked the balls. "Say, Dap, break 'em." But Dap pulled out his phone and started dialing as he took a seat by the bar. He couldn't shoot pool at a time like this. Bo just shook his head, and threw the pool stick on top of the table. Dap tried to act like he didn't even notice it but couldn't keep the laughter in. Tat was about to come home.

CHAPTER 4

━━━━

While Bo was on campus getting ready for his first college game, Dap was in Gonzales getting ready for the party that he was throwing for Tat tonight. He made sure he had everything ready to go, so after he watched the game, he could pick Tat up, and they could roll out. Tat was at home enjoying his freedom with his family after being released earlier. His mom told him that Dap was coming by to pick him up, and if this was the same Dap from years ago, Tat knew this would be one long night.

Dap pulled up to Tat's crib and made a few calls before getting out of his Cadillac. He wanted to make sure that everything was going as planned. The last thing he wanted to do was let Tat down. He walked through the yard and raised his hand to ring the doorbell, but he was still a few steps from the door when it opened swiftly.

"What took you so long, bruh?" Tat gave Dap one of the biggest hugs he'd ever gotten in his life. "Say, bruh, thank you for everything. The money, letters, pictures, visits. Everything. Mama told me how you would stop by and check on her. Nobody else did any of that. I love you for that." Dap was never the type to show emotions. He felt some tears trying to form, but he wasn't having that.

"Man, fuck all that. We ain't 'bout to do all of this emotional shit. You home now, pimpin. Let's go get twisted."

"Here you go. Light this shit up. This ain't no regular weed either." Dap gave Tat a perfectly rolled blunt as they headed out to a hotel right off of I-10. Tat took a sniff and made a sour face.

"What the fuck is this? This shit smells super loud."

Dap grins. "I wish you coulda seen the look on your face just now. It's called Sour Diesel. We ain't had none of this back in the gap. And don't be tryna roll up no papers. We smoke blunts. Got that?" Tat doesn't answer. He lights the blunt and takes a puff. He tries to hold it in but can't. Dap laughs at him as he coughs. "Take ya time, bruh. We got a lotta this shit. And I don't want you to get fucked up to the point that you can't enjoy yourself tonight. Shiiiiiiddd, it's about to go down!"

CHAPTER 5

W hat the fff…?" Tat couldn't even finish his thought. The first thing that caught his attention was the aroma that exploded into his nostrils as soon as he stepped into the hotel suite. It wasn't the same thing they smoked on the way. This was also strong but different. He locked eyes with a gorgeous brown-skinned beauty who was responsible for the blend of purple smoke and Ed Hardy for women. She was dressed like a principal at a high school. Tat couldn't believe how beautiful she was. Tat was finally able to disengage from the stare-off to take a view of what he had just become a part of. He and Dap were the only males in the room. With eight females.

"Say, Dap, bruh? You doin' it like this?" Tat bobbed his head to the mellow groove playing on the portable CD player. "Damn, I'm happy to be a free man!"

"Ay, we 'bout to have a ménage e ten!" Dap signaled for two females who were lying in the bed with only panties on. "Y'all treat my man right." He walked away from the trio and took a seat on the sofa next to the brown beauty who'd caught Tat's attention just a few moments ago. She passed him the blunt of Purple Kush that she had been smoking. As he puffed, a gorgeous white girl took a seat in his lap. This was no regular white girl; she had serious ass. Most black girls didn't have an ass like hers. She kissed Dap all over his neck and removed his shirt. Then she kissed and nibbled all over his chest and shoulders as he smoked and allowed his right hand to explore the brown beauty's body as she perched on the arm of the chair. He needed both hands, so he closed his eyes and took one more long drag off the blunt and then held it in the air. And just like that the blunt was passed, making it obvious that this was his routine.

When Dap finally opened his eyes, there were two more females accompanying him and the original pair. He quickly glanced across the room to see if Tat was enjoying himself, and indeed he was. He was stroking one fair-skinned sister from the back while she licked a medium-toned beauty with a curly 'fro. Two other females were kissing and rubbing all over Tat, awaiting their turns.

Dap thought to himself, "Oh, yeah, he's enjoying himself." He smiled and gave his attention to the females who were crawling all over him. The two friends indulged in an all-night frenzy of pleasure with the eight lovely ladies. This would definitely be a night to remember.

CHAPTER 6

They were only two games into the season, and Bo was already being labeled a "special teams demon." He had eight total tackles, and the opponents seemed to have trouble getting up after every single one of them. Bo was sure to get some snaps on defense if he kept playing like that on special teams. However, it wouldn't be an easy task. LSU's two starting cornerbacks were both All-American seniors. Heck, he wasn't even playing as their backup yet. He was fifth on the depth chart, but everybody knows what a program like this is all about. The best of the best come to LSU to play football, and no matter how good you are, you have to earn your playing time. You have to force your way onto the field. As good as he was, Bo seemed to be improving every week. It was only a matter of time.

Bo also seemed to be taking his education very seriously. If he wasn't at football practice or at the facility, he was most likely in the corner of the library doing some school work. He knew how important it was to have something to fall back on if he didn't make it into the NFL for one reason or another. And disappointing his parents was certainly not an option. He was determined to graduate in four years. No excuses.

Bo hated General Chemistry I. He'd done well in high school chemistry, but it had always taken more of his time and attention than any other subject, including Calculus and Physics. The same could be said of college chemistry. He'd been staring into the pages of his textbook so long that his eyes were beginning to hurt. He closed his book and rubbed his eyes in an attempt to gain some relief.

"Excuse me. Do you mind if I sit here? I'm trying to avoid the crowded sections, and I need this outlet for my laptop." Bo removed the heels of his hands from his eyes and was simultaneously shocked and pleased at the beauty he was beholding.

"I don't mind at all. Go right ahead." He hadn't even been thinking of hooking up with females since he started college. It was all about playing football and getting an education, but this girl caught his attention like no one else had. She was much taller than average, and she wasn't wearing any makeup. No tight jeans or short skirt. She was a natural beauty with Gap sweats and a loose v-neck t-shirt. Her voice was sweet and sensual without any effort. Bo couldn't remember the last time a female had caught his attention like this.

"I'm about to leave anyway. This chemistry is killing me. Everything else is relatively easy, but this general chem has always been a challenge." He started gathering his things but kept glancing at the young lady without being obvious. Bo never approached girls. He'd always been particularly shy, certainly not what one would expect of a football standout, but he was feeling some kind of way just then.

"Hi. I'm Lebeau, freshman." He couldn't believe he'd actually introduced himself; he couldn't wait to tell Dap this one.

"Hi, I'm Tori, freshman." They shook hands and smiled shyly at each other. "Uhm, I'm actually pretty good at chemistry. I can tutor you if you like."

Bo wanted to thank God up close and personal for this moment. "I'd appreciate that very much. How much would it cost?"

"Well, let's see. As long as I don't have to deal with a crazy baby mama or girlfriend, no charge. I don't mind helping people. People help me from time to time, too. I just hate the drama, can't stand the drama." She looked at Bo in anticipation of an answer, but Bo was caught up in the moment. He was having visions that made him feel more like Dap than himself.

"Oh, I don't have any kids. And no girlfriend. It's only school and football for me. " His eyes went from her face to her perfect, perky breasts, and then down to her hips. Realizing it would be difficult to keep his mind off his new friend, Bo just shook his head.

"Are you okay?" Tori noticed that Bo was lost in thought. She laughed and gave Bo a pat on his back. "I'm gonna need you to focus and take tutoring seriously. Can you do that?"

Bo grinned and nodded. "Yes, ma'am. I can do that."

"Good." She gave Bo a thorough look over from his head to his toes. "We can start now if you like."

Bo simply smiled and unpacked the books, notebooks, and other supplies that he'd just recently packed.

CHAPTER 7

"Dap, you aint' gon believe this. I think I've me the finest, most beautiful female on campus. She volunteered to tutor me. You know I'm not the one to go out of my way to holla at a chick, man, but I couldn't help myself!" The excitement in Bo's tone was apparent. He hadn't mentioned anything about a female to Dap in a while.

"Awwww, shit. It's about damn time! You had me worried, buddy. So, did you hit? She got some good stuff? She hit the head? Spill it, bruh." Dap seemed to be even more excited than Bo. He had been wondering how long his friend was going to go without being with a woman.

And just like that, the glow on Bo's face turned to staleness. He knew Dap wouldn't like what he was about to say. "I didn't hit yet. We only meet at the library and talk and text each other. She's not like the average female. I'm tellin' you, bruh. She's focused. All she talks about is school and family. I think she's wifey material."

Dap stared at Bo in disbelief for what seemed to be an eternity before he finally let his friend have it. "You got to be fuckin' kidding me. You didn't smash, and you already calling her wifey material? Are you serious? Lemme tell you something. Them hoes know how to run game just like we run it. You know what? I ain't gon tell you nothing. I'mma see how long this bullshit last."

Dap's nerves had become really bad. He hated that Bo didn't see the world in the way he saw it. He began to wonder what Bo would do without him. He took an already rolled blunt and lit is as he shook his head at the naiveté of his friend.

But Bo wasn't done. "Why do you have to always be so damn negative? Just because I ain't sleepin' with all these chicks and hustlin' and packin' a pistol like you, that means I'm lame? I gotta do all that shit to be a man? You know more than me because I'm not like you? Look, you live your life how you wanna live yours and let me live mine."

Dap had never heard Bo go off like this before; he actually admired Bo for it. He still thought his friend was being naïve though. He watched Bo gaze into outer space with a frown on his face. "Ya nerves bad now? Here, hit this shit. It's gonna make it all better." He extended his arm as if offering Bo some weed, but he knew he wouldn't take it.

"Boy, fuck you!" They both laughed as the tension went away. "I'm serious though. All you need to do is have my back. I'm really digging this chick. You know it's some real shit if I'm telling you about it."

Bo went on and on about all of the things he liked about Tori, and now he wanted Dap to meet her. Dap just sat and listened and smoked his green leafy stuff.

"Well?" Bo was waiting to see what else Dap had to say about the situation. He hoped that his friend would understand why he felt the way he did about Tori.

"What the hell do you want me to say? You already know what you wanna do. If you like it; then I love it." His phone vibrated in his pocket. He pulled it out, and glanced at the screen. "I'mma holla at you later. I gotta make a run." Dap never stayed in one spot too long. If he wasn't with one of his many females, he was making money one way or another. He wasn't exactly what you would call a baller, but he certainly wasn't struggling. He had all types of hustles.

"Aight, bruh, but I'mma need you to be polite whenever you meet Tori. Cool?" Bo looked at Dap and waited for an answer.

Dap glanced at his friend for two or three long seconds and walked away without answering. Bo shook his head and went on about his business.

CHAPTER 8

Dap was well-known around Baton Rouge and the surrounding areas before he started attending Southern University, but although many of his college peers had heard of him, they had never seen him before. They simply couldn't put a name to a face. He liked it this way; he enjoyed being able to go places and do things without people really knowing who he was.

"Say, bruh, we gotta do that shit again." Tat was referring to the party that Dap had given him. He had no idea that Dap could pull off stuff like that.

"One of them broads looked like a straight up good girl, like all she do is go to work and church. I probably woulda tried to handcuff her if I'd met her before that night. Shit, I was on her more than all the other chicks.

She got that fiya for real. I gotta find her ass!" They both laughed.

"You and Bo killing me with the wifey and handcuff shit. You just got home. Enjoy yourself and kill all that serious shit. Live a little. Have some fun, man. Once you tie that knot, you can throw all that excitement out the window." A group of attractive young ladies walked by, some of them making eye contact with Dap and Tat. "See what I'm talking 'bout? Look around us, Tat. Look at all these fine ass chicks." They were walking through the student union on campus. This was Tat's first time on Southern's campus since he was a kid and he went to a football game with his mama. He certainly wasn't thinking about school at the moment.

"Who got some trees? I ain't smoked all day." Tat believed that marijuana keeps him calm and helps him to deal with bad memories and whatever issues he's dealing with. "They need to legalize that shit ASAP anyway!"

"I know a cat who keeps that purp. Let's go walk over there to the apartments." Dap led the way as they walked to the student housing.

Hearing the light knock at the door, Tiko walked to the door and glanced through the peephole. He recognized Dap, who had stopped by several times with another guy to cop some purp. He saw Dap as a cool, laid back brother. Although, he was kind of in the middle of something, he still opened the door. "This cat is harmless," Tiko thought to himself.

"Whuttup, yo. Y'all come in." He locked the door after Dap and Tat stepped inside. Tiko wasn't from Louisiana, but he had obviously gotten comfortable. Two bricks of compressed high-grade marijuana were on the coffee table in plain sight. Two duffle bags were on the floor next to an armchair. One of the bags wasn't zipped all the way making it easy to glimpse at the banded stacks of bills inside.

"Wushannin, Tiko? Lemme get an ounce of that purple." Dap went into his pocket and pulled out a roll of money with a rubber band around it. He noticed the bricks of weed on the table and the duffles by the chair. His heart began to beat faster; his mind went into overdrive, and then he saw the money peeking out one of the bags. His mind was made up in a snap. His eyes flicked up to Tat's to see if he'd also noticed everything. Tat gave Dap a simple nod, and Dap quietly put the money back into his pocket.

"Bitch, put yo hands up and don't move, not even a lil bit. If you try anything, I'mma blow ya fuckin' brains out." Dap held a 9mm firmly against the back of Tiko's head. He was ready for Tiko to make a wrong move. Instead, he placed the sandwich bag on the table with the weed he'd been about to prep for Dap, and he put his hands above his head. Tiko was afraid to utter a single word. Dap signaled for Tat to grab the weed and the duffles.

"Ay, go check out the other rooms. Look in the closets, the drawers, under the bed, between the mattresses, in shoeboxes. Check everything." It was clear to Tiko that Dap wasn't new to this. Today was no day to play the hero, so as he felt the cold steel at the back of his head, he simply watched as Tat stuff the bricks of marijuana into one of the bags before leaving the room.

"Lay down, nigga. Face down, on your stomach. Put yo hands behind ya head." Dap was in total control. Just as Tiko was getting on his knees, Tat came back into the room with two pistols and another duffle bag. He cocked one of the guns and tucked it at his waistline. He put the other gun into the bag and placed it next to the other two bags.

"Lemme go check the other room." He dashed out of the room once again. Tiko only heard Tat's voice this time. He didn't watch. He helplessly lay face down on the floor; he felt defeated.

"Say, bitch, if I even hear that you lookin' for me or even told somebody that I jacked you, I'mma kill you." Dap meant every word, and Tiko knew it.

"Let's go." Tat came back into the room with another bag. Dap didn't even ask what was in them. He nodded at Tat and then checked Tiko's pockets. He only had a phone, and Dap took it.

Dap thought about putting a bullet into the back of Tiko's head. "I oughtta kill you just because, bitch."

Tiko had been really quiet up until this point. "Nooooo, mannn! You got that. I'm takin' my loss. You ain't gotta kill me, man! I'm taking the loss like a man. Look, I'mma just leave B.R. Just don't kill me!"

"I think that's a damn good idea. Leave tonight. Not next week. Not tomorrow. Get the fuck outta Baton Rouge tonight." Dap still wanted to do something to make sure Tiko knew he meant business. He struck Tiko behind the head with the pistol, knocking him unconscious. The two friends each grabbed two bags and calmly left the scene.

CHAPTER 9

"Now this is what I call a come up!" Dap sat at the table in his apartment with Tat sitting across from him. "This is the biggest lick I've ever hit. It's not even comparable to the others."

On the table was $150,000 cash money, two pounds of purple Kush marijuana, and five kilos of cocaine. Dap and Tat stared at the contents in amazement.

"Did I ever mention to you that I'm glad to be free again?" They both laughed. "So what do we do with all of this shit?" Tat didn't feel comfortable hustling because he'd been off the scene for far too long. He didn't know who was running what block or street. He didn't want anything to do with selling drugs at the moment.

"We split the money. $75,000 a piece. Make sure you stash that shit. You don't even need it right now. We gon' smoke the purp and sell a little of it and use that for our party and bullshit money. I'mma get rid of the cocaine. I ain't breaking shit down. I should be able to get rid of all five kilos at once. If not, I'll just sell them separately. But, like I said, I ain't breaking them down. People get caught when they get greedy. If I can't get what I want for them, I'mma just hold on to them until I can get what I want. We shouldn't have any problems though. I know who to go to first. And whatever I get for the cocaine we gon' split that fifty-fifty also." He grabbed a cigarillo and tossed it to Tat. "Roll up. Lemme make a call right quick."

Dap called up a guy he grew up with. Big Dawg was a well-known drug dealer who was also well-respected. It's no surprise that he was running things in his area. His brother had all of Baton Rouge on lock before he received a fifteen year federal sentence. It's rumored that he has police on his payroll and if anyone harms a hair on his head, the whole BR is gonna ride for him.

"What up, Big Dawg!" Although the two were childhood friends, they rarely saw each other. Still they were pretty cool and had lots of respect for each other. "You think you can meet me at Geno's tonight? I gotta run some shit down to you."

"Whassup, Dap! Yeah, I can pass over there around eight. I'mma be in the area." Big Dawg didn't even ask what it was about. They both knew not to talk details over the phone. And he knew all about Dap. He wondered if Dap was trying to be a major player in the dope game now.

"Aight. Bet. See you then, homie." Dap hung up and looked at Tat with a devilish grin. "Pass that shit!"

Dap made it to Geno's at seven-thirty. He wanted to be there already when Big Dawg got there, and he didn't bring Tat along because he didn't want Big Dawg to feel uncomfortable or cautious for any reason.

As always, Geno greeted him as soon as he spotted him. "What's going on, young blood! You solo tonight? I see Bo is cuttin' up on that field. That's a bad boy!"

"Yeah, he's as focused as they come. He won't be in here anytime soon. You know how he gets during football season. Annndd he's all in love and shit." They both laughed as Geno signaled for a barmaid to bring Dap his favorite drink. "I'mma go chill by the bar and catch a lil SportsCenter for a minute or two."

Dap wasn't sitting for five minutes when Big Dawg walked in. His eyes were glued to the flat screen TV behind the bar when he heard Geno greet Big Dawg.

After speaking to a few people, Big Dawg spotted Dap and made his way to the bar. These two guys are cut from the same cloth. Fairly quiet and humble, but as brave as they come. Well-respected in the streets. Loved by the ladies. And they had both decided at an early age that being broke was not an option.

"Whoa nah, Dap." Big Dawg spoke and climbed onto the empty bar stool next to Dap. They gave each other a pound. "What da bidnizz is?" Big Dawg was never the kind to procrastinate, always straight to the point.

"Whassup, homie? I'm good. Life is good. I appreciate you meeting me on such short notice. Check this out. I hit a nice lil lick, and I have something you might be interested in. You know I've dabbled in the dope game from time to time, but it's not my thang, ya dig. And I know you doing your thang, so before I get out there on the block and fuck with anybody else or compete with you in any kind of way, I'd rather let you get it for cheap." Dap felt that this approach was a wise one and it would be hard for Big Dawg to refuse. He certainly had Big Dawg's attention.

"Hunh, bruh. What you came up on like that, homie?" Big Dawg was expecting Dap to be interested in purchasing some weight, but instead, Dap is trying to sell off some weight. This really caught him off guard.

"I got five bricks of white. I have a lil sample for you right here. Check it out." Dap reached in his pocket and pulled out a small bag of cocaine and handed it to Big Dawg without being obvious.

Big Dawg took the sample bag and let out a childish grin. "Five bricks? It's been a really long time since I scored as little as five bricks."

He didn't know if the look on Dap's face was one of offense or disappointment. Or both.

"Dap, if I ain't coming back with fifty bricks, I ain't even taking that ride, but I like ya grind. I fucks withcha. Lemme see

what you working with." He opened the bag and stuck a pinky finger in it to sample the product." Yeah, you got some official shit right here. I tell you what. I'll give you...$75.000 for all five. Now you can make way more than that if you break that shit down. Or you can get off each brick one at a time. But then you would be taking major risks to make that kinda money. And honestly, you ain't doing me any favors. I would be doing you one though, so it's $75,000. Take it or leave it."

Dap looked Big Dawg eye to eye for nearly ten seconds before he finally spoke up. "Exactly. So $75,000 it is."

CHAPTER 10

Dap didn't feel too good about having all this money and not sharing the wealth with Bo, so he and Tat decided to take thirty thousand dollars each from the cocaine sale and give the remaining fifteen thousand to Bo. Although Bo lived a completely different lifestyle and didn't contribute to the stick-up, they wanted to show him some love.

"Catch, bitch!" Dap threw three rolls of money to Bo at once, and Bo missed all three. "What the fuck, bruh?! How you gon' play football and can't catch? So you gon have a bunch of tackles and no interceptions, hunh?" Dap chuckled as he slung himself down onto Bo's bed.

Bo slowly picked up the money, examining the rolls. "How much is this?" His eyes shifted to Dap.

"Fifteen stacks. Don't spend it all in one place." Dap didn't want to get into the when, where, how, and who thing. "Why you ain't startin' yet? You killing shit on special teams. You've been solid whenever they put you in nickel and dime packages. I know you kicking ass in the weight room. They need to quit bullshittin' and give your more playing time."

"You keep forgetting that we have two All-American cornerbacks. I ain't trippin'. I like my position. All I can do is wreak havoc whenever I step on that field. And we're winning. I won't complain." As soon as Bo stopped talking, his attention went back to the fifteen grand in his hand.

"Nobody had to lose their life behind this, huhh?" Before Bo could finish questioning Dap, someone started knocking on his door. He quickly stuffed the money into his pockets and walked to the door and opened it.

"Heeyyy, baby. I wasn't expecting you." Tori usually called Bo before she stopped by but she didn't this time. She walked in but froze when she saw Dap sitting on Bo's bed. It was as though she had seen a ghost. "I'm sorry, baby. I didn't know you had company." Tori took a couple of steps backwards and was about to turn around when Dap spoke up.

"No, ma. It's okay. I was just leaving." Dap stood up and started walking towards the door, which was where Bo and Tori were.

Tori was obviously nervous. Still, Bo didn't want to be rude. In fact, he had been wanting Dap to meet her. "Sweetheart, I'd like you to meet my best friend, Daron. Daron, this is my girl, Tori."

Dap extended his hand to shake Tori's hand. "Hi, I'm Dap. Please don't call me, Daron." He noticed how the palm of her hand was sweating and that she was trembling a little. Dap wondered what here problem was. She quickly took her hand back and looked away.

"Man, I'mma get outta here and let you do your thang." He gave Bo a pound and then looked at Tori.

"Nice meeting you," he said; then he left the dorm and closed the door. He stood outside in the hallway, mind racing.

"Where do I know this girl from?" He tried to figure out why Tori was so nervous. She clearly knew him, but he had been around the block more than a few times and had met hundreds of women. But he'd remember her soon enough.

CHAPTER 11

———

"Is something wrong?" Bo wanted to ignore Tori's strange reaction to seeing Dap, but he just couldn't.

"Not really. I just expected you to be alone. I didn't tell you I was stopping by because I wanted to surprise you." Tori wanted Bo to forget about her reaction to seeing Dap. She wanted to forget it also. But did Dap even recognize her?

"To surprise me? What's the special occasion?" Bo was confused. *What could this be about? She sure didn't have a gift in her hand or anything?*

Tori walked up to Bo and put her arms around him, squeezing him tight. "You treat me so good, Bo. You take your tutoring sessions seriously. You haven't rushed me into sex. I really appreciate you." Her hands began to glide up and down Bo's back. Here head relaxed on his chest, and they were both quiet for several still minutes.

Bo broke the silence. "Ummmm...so, what's the surprise?" He awaited a response for what seemed an eternity. Finally Tori removed her face from his chest.

"Put on some music, baby. Something slow. Something smooth." She grinned as Bo gave her a puzzled look.

"Ummm...okay. You like Beyonce'? I'mma put on her Pandora station. Cool?" Bo grabbed his phone and found the station he was looking for. He docked it on the speaker system, and seconds later, Beyonce's "Dance for You" began to stream through the dorm room.

Now have a seat, mister. I need for you to relax." She loved that song, and there weren't better lyrics for what she had in store for him. Tori was already deep into the song by the time Bo sat on his bed. Hypnotizing Bo with her eyes, she stood right in front of him, gyrating her hips smoothly and slowly to the melody. She allowed her hands to explore her body then removed her t-shirt, fluidly pulling it over her head to fully expose her lacy, see-through bra. Her arousal was evident from the hardness of her nipples as they poked at the lace.

Bo sat in amazement as Tori removed her bra, displaying her perfect, perky breasts. He watched her squeeze them together, and his excitement increased. Tori noticed the bulge in his sweatpants.

Oh, are you happy to see me?" She smiled and bit her lip. "Let's see how happy you get now." She began to unbutton her skinny jeans as she stared into Bo's eyes. As she unzipped the black denim and slid them down her slim, strong legs, Bo grew more and more anxious.

Tori was not wearing any panties, and Bo was in heaven. He watched as she massaged her inner thighs and her cleanly shaved flower. She took a few steps forward and put her arms around him.

Bo couldn't take it anymore; he had been patient long enough. He grabbed Tori's waist and jerked her closer. He placed soft, subtle kisses across her abdomen before moving up to her breasts.

Tori moaned in pleasure. She took one of Bo's hands and placed it between her legs. She was soaked. Bo took that as a sign that it had been a while since she'd engaged in any sexual activity. He just kicked back and let Tori do her thing. She was in control, and he enjoyed it.

CHAPTER 12

There wasn't much activity on Southern's campus. Most students were gone for the weekend or inside the dorm rooms relaxing. A nice cool autumn breeze blew along the Mississippi River as the sun began to set.

Dap sat patiently in his Cadillac as he stalked Tiko's apartment. Despite of what some people believed, he had never taken another man's life. But that was about to change. He warned Tiko.

He wasn't sure if Tiko was inside alone though. The thought of having to kill innocent bystanders made him uncertain of his mission. He noticed the silhouette of someone walking past the living room window. Scoping out the parking lot, Dap climbed out of his car with a loaded 380 caliber chrome-plated pistol. He planned on tossing the small handgun into the river as soon as he did what he had come to do.

The sun finally disappeared. As Dap walked toward the entrance of the apartment, the door opened unexpectedly. He raised the 380 in anticipation of filling Tiko's chest with hot lead, but what he saw almost made him drop the pistol onto the concrete.

A woman who appeared to be in her fifties approached the doorway. Not noticing the young man dressed in all black, she dragged a full garbage bag to the threshold.

He placed the firearm in his back pocket as the woman closed and locked the door. "Excuse me, ma'am. Who do I need to talk to about renting one of these apartments?" Dap was used to talking himself out of bad situations.

"Hi, young man. There's usually someone in the office around this time, but they leave early on Fridays. Shoot, everybody goes into a totally different mode on Friday's around here. Just go to the office before six p.m. on Monday, and they'll fix you up. There were some vacancies here, but it seems full now, and I don't know what the waiting list is like. The guy who was staying in this first floor unit right here just left last night though.

Said he had some kinda emergency and told the manager he had to leave. Said he definitely wouldn't be back." As she referred to Tiko, she pointed back to the apartment that she had just cleaned.

"Thank you so much, ma'am. Is this trash? I can bring it to the dumpster for you." Dap grabbed the bag before the lady could answer.

"Ohhhh, thank you so much young man. We need more of your kind around here." She smiled brightly as Dap sauntered off with the bag of trash.

Dap took a deep breath as he walked away. He felt relieved because he didn't really want to take Tiko's life, but he certainly would have. He was just playing the hand that life dealt him. No father. He couldn't depend on his mother for anything. Being on his own since his early teens, he depended on hustles and schemes. It was all he knew.

CHAPTER 13

Although he appreciated the fact that he made it to college, Dap had never taken the time to actually enjoy the college experience. It was all about the next chick he could sleep with or his next hustle.

His mind was somewhat at ease now that he knew Tiko had left town. He decided to take a walk around campus and have a little time to himself. As he walked past the different halls and dormitories, he wondered if his mother even cared about him. The only time he ever sees her is at family gatherings. She's never home when he stops by to see her. She never calls. He thought it would cease to bother him one day but he couldn't help but wonder how a parent, especially a mother, could not even care for their very own seed.

He didn't want to walk anymore. He needed for all of the emotions he felt at the moment to go away. There was a bench in front of a nearby hall. Dap decided to take a seat there. He stared into the darkness, tears flowing from his eyes.

"Look at me." Dap shook his head and wiped the tears away. He pulled an already rolled blunt out of his pocket and lit it. As he smoked, more tears rolled down his face. The sound of footsteps snapped Dap out of his trans. A gorgeous beauty walked in his direction. He quickly wiped his face again. But instead of putting the blunt out he simply held it in his hand, keeping it out of plain sight.

"No need in hiding it. You can smell that stuff on the other side of the campus. And if the wrong campus security sees you they gone trip." The young lady said what she had to say and walked right past Dap. She didn't even look at him.

"Good looking out, ma. But you don't think you need to be walking with a friend or something? I know this is a college campus and all but still…. It's dark. And people are crazy these days. You never can be too safe, ya know." Dap didn't bother to hide his weed anymore. He took a long drag as he watched the stranger walk up the steps in front of the hall.

She recognized his voice. The young lady reached the top of the steps and turned around. "Daron? You gotta be kidding me. I can't believe that you're here on campus on a Friday night. It's about to rain cats, dogs, horses, and giraffes. Then again, you're probably meeting one of your little skeezers over here." She snickered and stared at Dap, waiting on a comeback from him.

"What the…..wow. Really? You seem to think you know a lot about me. And I have no clue who you are." Dap leaned forward and used the concrete to put out the blunt.

"I know more about you than you think. You're not even from Baton Rouge. You're from Convent. Y'all moved here when you were a kid. You and Bo have been like brothers ever since you moved here. You drive a Cadillac. You've slept with a thousand women. You have a jacked-up attitude that caused you to miss out on a scholarship to play basketball." She giggled as Dap looked at her quietly, trying to figure out who she is and how she knew him.

"And you have a reputation as a gangsta. But I'm not impressed. And I'm not afraid of yo ass. I wish you would try to play games with me." She now had a serious look on her face.

Dap smiled. He couldn't help it. He liked her feistiness. Finally, he stood up and walked up the steps toward her. "How do you know all my business, Miss Thang? And I ain't bang no thousand chicks."

"Okay. My bad. Nine hundred and ninety-nine." They both laughed out loud. "I'm Tamara. I'm Slim's little cousin. You don't remember me but I sure remember you. I see you every time you go to Convent. You never paid any attention to me because you're always busy chasing those easy hoes who give their stuff away to everybody."

The smile on Dap's face disappeared. "I hope you stop saying shit like that. I probably never paid you any attention because of Slim. He's like family. So his family is like my family. See…I can tell that you think you have all the answers. And what the hell are you doing way over here on this side of campus by yourself at night? Interrupting my smoke session and shit. You better be lucky you're Slim's little cousin." Dap stood right in front of Tamara. He was so tall that her eyes were level with his stomach.

"First of all, I left my I.D. in the computer lab and I came back to get it. Second of all, I got something for anybody who decides to try me." Tamara reached inside her small purse and pulled out a taser.

"This is for small matters .But I have something else for bigger matters. She placed the taser back inside her purse and pulled out a small pistol.

"This is for the pervs and jackasses who think it's a game." She held a small 25 caliber hand gun in her palm for a few seconds before placing it back inside her purse.

"Well I'll be damn. Madea goes to college. I was gonna ask if you'd like for me to walk you back to your dorm after you get your I.D. But, shit, can YOU walk ME to your dorm?" Laughter erupted from the pair as Tamara went inside the building to retrieve her I.D. and Dap waited outside.

Dap was attracted to Tamara in every way. She had hypnotizing eyes and long, natural hair that hung to her shoulders. Her smooth, butter pecan skin was flawless. She had hips and ass that made men AND women drool. But he couldn't go after her. She wasn't the average female. She deserved love and wouldn't settle for anything other than that. And he simply wasn't looking for love.

"Got it! " Tamara held her I.D. card in her hand as she burst through the doors. "Now let me walk your scary ass to my dorm before some goons catch you slippin."

"Look, you ain't gone be making fun of me all the time. I'm letting you know that right now." The couple started their journey across campus. Dap took out what was left of his blunt.

Tamara was on his case before he could get to his lighter. "And you ain't gone be smoking that stink shit around me. I'm letting you know that right now." Dap knew her tone that she wasn't joking. Still, he lit the blunt.

As soon as the blunt was lit, Tamara stopped walking. Dap gave her a puzzled look. "Are you serious? You gotta be kidding me."

"Does it look like I'm playing? I don't mind walking alone." Her hands were on her hips now. She didn't budge as she watched Dap contemplate his next move.

Finally, he shook his head and flicked the remainder of the blunt onto the ground. Tamara's eyes were glued to his. She bit her bottom lip and tried not to smile too hard.

"You're killing me." Dap felt defeated as he waited for Tamara to catch up with him.

"Thank youuuuuuuuu. You are such a gentleman." Tamara playfully shoved him in the back.

"AND you're violent. I can't deal." They laughed and flirted as they walked under the moon-lit sky.

Tamara didn't invite Dap inside her dorm room. And he didn't ask to go in. Instead, they sat outside and talked for hours. This was a first for Dap but he welcomed this pleasant surprise. When they finally went their separate ways, they were both satisfied. Happy. Smiling. The time they spent together was better than any feeling that sex could bring. It was priceless.

CHAPTER 14

Bo's relationship with Tori was getting more and more serious with each passing week. She attended all of his games and wore a jersey bearing his number. He even brought her home to meet his parents. Although Mr. and Mrs. Johnson really like his ex, April, they are pleased that he has found happiness with someone. They had begun to worry that he would be scarred for life with April leaving him.

He sure didn't let his personal life effect his play on the football field. Bo was inserted into the starting lineup due to injuries to other corner backs and he has been turning heads. His LSU Tigers were ranked #2 in the nation with one more game to play before competing for the SEC title. This was a dream come true.

Bo hadn't talked to Dap in a couple of weeks and decided to give him a call. "So, how many trips have your nasty ass taken to the clinic so far? Got about two or three babies on the way?" They have always teased each other about their differences. And Bo don't expect any changes in Dap anytime soon.

"Damn, Bo. Why you gotta hurt my feelings like that? You know all I do is go to class and stay inside like a good boy." They laughed.

"So, are you actually going to class and shit? I know you have the brains to make it through college but I also know the main reason you're in school. And plus you're still in your back yard. Not a good recipe for success in my opinion." Bo hoped that he didn't offend his friend. But he felt the need to be brutally honest for once.

"Well, believe it or not, Mr. LSU, I've been going to class and doing pretty decent. I got all A's and B's for mid-terms and I'm sure that's what I'm gonna finish with." Dap spoke about his grades as though they weren't a big deal. Bo was relieved and a bit surprised.

"Awwww shit! That's what I'm talking about! I'm surprised but damn I'm happy to hear that. So what's up with you and the females? How are the ladies treating you?" Bo just knew that he was about to hear about some wild college sex party.

Dap immediately thought of Tamara. He had been seeing her every day. His mind wandered off for a minute as he held the phone in silence.

"Dap! What the hell are you doing, bruh?" Bo wondered if something was wrong.

"Man, you are not gonna believe this." Dap's voice was calm. It was much different from what Bo had gotten used to over the years.

"Oh shit! You done fell in love with one of those old ass professors! You've been slangin that mule to an old ass lady in exchange for good grades!" Bo was weak from laughing.

"Look how crazy. I'm not sure if you remember Slim from Convent. Well, his cousin, Tamara, goes to Southern and we've been kickin it. I mean kickin it hard." Dap took a deep breath and tried not to make the obvious too obvious.

Bo removed his phone from his ear and looked at it. Confused, he put the phone back to his ear. "Hold up. Is this the same dude who seems to have issues with me chillin with Tori? Is this really my life-long ace? I can't believe what I'm hearing. Whatever happened to smashing chicks from all over the U.S.? I mean…I applaud you. I'm just curious what brought the change." Bo was actually excited. He always worried about Dap and his wild, unpredictable ways. He didn't want his best friend to go to prison, get killed, or deal with baby mama drama. Maybe Dap finally got the picture.

"She's different, bruh. Everything about her is positive. She's a natural beauty. She's jazzy, classy, intelligent, family - oriented. She has morals. She has street sense too! She's a complete female. I've been seeing her every day for a couple of weeks now." Dap finally went silent.

"Dammmmmmmmn! I've never heard you talk like this before. That girl must got that good good!" Bo's chuckling didn't last long once he realized he was chuckling alone.

"I don't know if it's good. I didn't get any. I didn't even try. All we ever do is talk and chill. We do school work and study together. She tells me about God and how she wants me to go to church with her. Bo, I've never met anybody like her in my life." Dap felt himself getting soft.

"But anyway, I see you got a starting spot now. I knew it wouldn't take long. You don't belong on the bench. You're a natural at that shit. All I know is I want 2 tickets to the title game."

"Awwww, hell no! You just gone switch it up on me like that? Classic Dap. Okay. Yeah, I'm starting now. But look, I gotta go. We gone finish this convo A.S.A.P." Bo had to go to the gym for his evening work-out.

"Cool. I'mma holla." As soon as his call with Bo ended, Dap called Tamara.

CHAPTER 15

Dap had never gone out of his way to put a smile on a female's face before. But Tamara has a firm grip on that heart of his. He cooked dinner and had a bottle of Moscato on chill. Two scented candles were placed on the table, ready to burn. Musiq Soulchild sang a smooth, calming ballad that traveled from the stereo speakers.

Then came the anticipated knock at the door. Dap sprayed on a little Issey Miyake and made his way down the hallway. He took a few seconds to light the candles and finally made it to the door.

"Hey, gorgeous. Come on in. Let me take your jacket." Tamara stepped inside the apartment and gave Dap a hug before allowing him to remove her jacket. This candlelight dinner would be their first date.

Tamara had on an elegant, satin dress that hugged every curve of her frame. Dap couldn't take his eyes off of her.

"Come and have a seat at the table, ma." He held her hand and led the way to the dining room. Like a gentleman, he pulled out a chair for Tamara.

"Thank you. I must say that I'm impressed. Very neat and clean apartment, candlelight, perfect music, and something smells good. Yeah, I'm impressed." Tamara didn't really know what to expect. But Dap had blown her away so far. This can't be the same Dap that she had heard so much about over the years.

"I'll be right back." Dap leaned forward and gave Tamara an innocent kiss on her left cheek. His cologne penetrated her nostrils. She closed her eyes as chills traveled down her spine.

Dap disappeared into the kitchen and returned seconds later with two plates, each covered with a steak, potatoes, and broccoli covered with cheese and chopped ham. Tamara watched in amazement as he placed the plates on the table. He made another quick trip to the kitchen to grab the wine and two glasses. He opened the bottle of Moscato and filled both glasses.

"I know you didn't cook this yourself." The smile on Tamara's face gave Dap the confirmation he eagerly awaited. He wanted to make a lasting impression and he felt that the evening couldn't possibly get any better.

After they ate, Dap led Tamara to the living room sofa. They were both full in wanted to get comfortable and relax.

"We can watch a movie or just listen to music and chill. Your choice, ma." Dap was sure to keep Tamara in a comfort zone. He didn't even want to bring up sex. He tried not to think about it but she was simply too stunning in that dress.

"Let's just keep the music on. The vibe is so right and I wanna keep it just like this. So keep the music on and keep the candles burning. What other music do you have?" Tamara was obviously comfortable, getting up to check out the stack of cds on top of the entertainment center.

"I have pretty much everything that came out the last few years. The stack you have now is all R&B. That's neo-soul next to it. You can put on whatever you like, sweetheart." Dap's eyes were glued to Tamara's butt. He couldn't believe that he hadn't noticed her all that time. "Wow. And the surprises just keep coming." Tamara turned around with her hand on her hip and smiled as she shook her head.

"What?" Dap had no clue what she was talking about.

"Frank Ocean. You listen to Frank Ocean? Hard ass, street ass Dap listens to Frank Ocean? Never would've guessed it in a million years." Tamara didn't know what to make of it. Most guys she knew didn't listen to Frank Ocean. At least they didn't admit it.

"So I'm not supposed to listen to his music because he's gay? Let me tell you something, darlin'. What he does in his own free time is his own business. I like good music, and the dude knows how to make some good music. His CD is full of hits. It's a damn classic. As for my view on gays in general, I treat them like I treat everybody else. Shit, who am I to judge them? As long as they respect me, I'm gonna respect them. I mean, I have gay relatives. That's still my people, you know?" Silence ruled the room as Dap took a sip from his glass.

Then he said, "But I ain't gon be ride around blasting that shit from my speakers with my boys in the car with me!" They laughed so hard that their stomachs began to hurt.

Finally, Tamara decided on a CD to play. The first track from R. Kelly's 12 Play blasted from the speakers.

"Your body is definitely calling me," Dap whispered to himself as he watched Tamara make her way back to him. She sat next to him on the sofa and put her head on his shoulder.

"What's wrong, love? You okay?" Dap sensed that something was bothering her.

"Nothing is wrong. Everything is right." Tamara lifted her head from Dap's shoulder and found his lips. They had never kissed like this before, but Dap welcomed it. Tamara felt herself getting moist. She had only experienced sex a few times with her boyfriend from high school, and although she liked Dap a lot, they were not in a serious relationship. That meant that she could not let things get out of hand. She forced her lips away from Dap's.

"Daron, I'm confused. I've heard so much about you. Yet you show me a side of you that I never knew existed. Why do you treat me differently from those other females?" Tamara was sitting up and looking straight into Dap"s eyes now.

"You're the only female who I feel deserves this type of treatment from me. How can I treat a woman like a queen if she only wants me because I was the star of the basketball team or because she thinks I have money?

73

How can I respect a female who gives me some the first time we meet? You're the only female who ever asked me about my background. You're the first one to talk about God to me. No woman had ever invited me to church before, and you see the good in me. You aren't here for my money; you have your own car and apartment. You sincerely want to know me. That's why it's so easy for me to treat you like a queen." Dap meant every word he spoke. Tears rolled down Tamara's cheeks as the words soothed her soul.

"You are truly everything I want in a man, and I'm not afraid to say that I'm falling for you. But I'm beaucoup cautious because I don't wanna get hurt. I know you have a past, and I'm not gonna judge you because of it. However, I have to look out for myself. Do you know your HIV status? What about other STDs? I've only been with one guy, but I still get tested twice a year. I have my paperwork, too." Tamara hoped she hadn't messed the night up by bringing that up, but she wanted Dap to know where she stood and what needed to happen to take their relationship to the next level.

"No, I don't. Never got tested and nobody ever asked me to take one, but I guess I'll be taking one soon." He pulled Tamara to him and cradled her in his arms.

"You are so amazing, Daron. I'm so glad I left my ID in that building that night." Tamara felt loved and adored as well as admired and respected.

Dap no longer cared about how many women he could sleep with. All he cared about now was the woman he was holding in his arms. He didn't really understand how he had set out to end a life that night but ended up crossing paths with someone who would ultimately change his life. He never complained when life seems to be dealing him bad cards. And now he was cherishing the winning hand he had received.

CHAPTER 16

"Bo, I need a favor. I need a HUGE favor." Dap knew that he would be able to catch his friend in his dorm room today. Bo was getting as much rest as he could before LSU's matchup with the Florida Gators in the SEC title game.

"You came over here just to ask me for a favor? You couldn't just call me? I can tell this is gonna be some bullshit." Bo hoped that Dap didn't plan on robbing a student or anything of that nature.

"It's not anything like that. I need you to come with me to take an HIV test. I'm too spooked to go by myself. I'm already nervous, bruh. You know my history." Dap started to pace back and forth in the small room.

"Damn, don't tell me. Some chick that you banged got that shit?" Bo hoped this wasn't the case, but he just had that feeling.

"Nahhhh, man. Tamara's ready to take it to the next level, and she wants me to get tested. I don't even know my status. And now that I care enough to find out, I'm scared as shit." Dap continued to wear a hole in Bo's carpet with his insistent pacing.

"Okay, I got you, homie. But try not to get worked up about it. You're as healthy as a horse. You're fine, man. You wanna go today? We gotta go right now before they close. There's a walk-in clinic right off of Highland Road. Let's go." There was no way that Bo was going to turn down a chance to be there for his best friend. He realized how much Tamara meant to Dap, and Dap's life seemed to be changing for the better. Bo was proud of his boy.

"See, that wasn't so bad." Bo was trying to brighten things up a bit. Dap had been quiet ever since they had left the clinic.

"Bo, do you know how many chicks I've had unprotected sex with? I know you don't know 'cause I don't know. Everybody's always talking about HIV and AIDS cases in Baton Rouge. Now look at my dumb ass." Dap spoke as if he knew he was HIV positive.

"Stop it, bruh. You're talking crazy. You act like you got the results back and you're positive. Chill yo ass out." Bo turned his music up and focused on the highway.

Dap's phone began to ring. It was Tat. Bo and Tat hadn't had a chance to kick it and catch up yet.

"What up, Tat. Where are you?" Dap figured it would be a good time to come together with his two best friends.

"At the crib? Cool. I'm about to come fuck with you." Dap was finally putting his worries about the test aside.

"You wanna go holla at Tat? I know you haven't seen him since he got out. He looks the same. He's just learned his lesson, too. He ain't tryna get caught up in no more bullshit."

"Hell yeah! Let's go pick that fool up. Is he by his mama's crib?" Bo was excited to finally be seeing Tat again.

"Yeah. That's where he's at. She still got that house off Sherwood."

They pulled up to Tat's mother's house to find him sitting on the step and smoking a blunt.

"Man, you still look the same! Whassup, boi!" Bo gave Tat a big hug.

"Shit, I'm just glad to be home. Other than my family, I only hang with that nigga next to you. That's the only nigga that held it down for me while I was gone. If it wasn't for that nigga…"

"Damn, Tat! How many times you gon say nigga? Do you have any idea how crazy that sounds?" Dap couldn't stand to hear the n-word or even curse words repeated constantly. He felt it was a sign of ignorance.

"Say, bruh, I'm just saying." Tat was offended; Bo and Dap could see it on his face. He was just trying to explain to Bo that Tat was a true friend.

"I know what you're tryna say, Tat. But what Dap is tryna say is that you don't have to use that particular word to make your point. And yes, we all say it sometimes, but we shouldn't say it at all." It didn't take long for Bo to get the impression that Tat was institutionalized. And just as Bo was thinking that, Tat started again.

"And see them fuckin' white folks: they don't care about us, bruh. All of them bitches racist." Tat was obviously having a moment.

"Tat, I'ma say this and then we gon end this conversation. Forget about all that bullshit you experienced in jail. You're free now. And you don't even know enough white people to say all white folks are racist. I can think back as far as first grade when Mrs. Scott, our white teacher, went above and beyond for us black students. Remember her? I'm talking about buying us clothes, and giving us snack money, and giving extra attention to all the kids who needed it. And white folks are all around you. Get used to it and learn how to coexist with them. White people are not the enemy. The sooner you realize that, the better. Now, lemme hit that blunt 'cause you got me all out of my element." Dap didn't want to talk anymore, and Tat just passed him the blunt.

Bo's phone vibrated in his pocket, and he slipped it out to view the screen. It was Tori. She was at the mall and wondering if Bo was gonna pass by. Of course he would.

"Ay, y'all wanna pass by the mall when y'all finish burnin'?" Bo was sure the fellas wouldn't mind.

"Yeah, let's roll." Dap usually went to the mall alone, but he'd make an exception today for his friends.

I'm down. Legggo!" Tat was more than glad to ride out with Bo and Dap. These were two guys he knew he could learn a lot from, even if it was tough medicine sometimes.

As soon as they made it to the mall, Bo texted Tori to get her location. She was in Lady Foot Locker. "Let's run by Lady Foot Locker real quick. My girl is over there and I just wanna holla real fast before she leaves." Bo expected a derogatory remark from Dap, but his friend didn't say a word.

As they approached their first destination in the mall, Tat started hitting excitedly on Dap's chest with the back of his hand. "Dap! Dap! That her right there, ole girl from the party. I knew I

would see her again somewhere." Tat's whisper was so loud that the party girl heard him Dap looked at the chick, and then his jaw dropped. His mouth was open, but he couldn't get any words out. He turned to look at Bo and saw the confused look on his other friend's face.

"You mean her right there?" Bo pointed to the young lady in question as they continued to approach the sneaker store.

She was stuck. Paralyzed. Why was this happening to her? She wanted to scream, but no words came out. She wanted to run away, but she was stuck to that very spot.

"Yeah. I'm talkin' 'bout her. You know her, too, Bo?" Tat was lost. He had no clue what was going on.

"You gotta be kidding me. That's Bo's girlfriend, Tori." It all came back to Dap in a rush of images. Dap realized that Tori had recognized him in Bo's dorm room that day, and he knew he didn't recognize her as the same female from the party because he had been super high and Tat had kept her on lock the entire night.

High or sober, Tat didn't have that same problem. He'd been waiting to see her again, but he never would have guessed that it would be under these awful circumstances.

The three friends stopped directly in front of Tori. "Well, hello, Tori. I guess you don't need an introduction to my boy, Tat. It seems that you already know him very well." Even though Bo was not making a scene and his voice held a normal volume, the anger in his hard tone was evident.

"I thought I had a lady, a decent female, someone I could have a future with. But you ain't nothin' but a common slut." Bo's blood was boiling. He wanted to say so many mean and degrading things to her, but he held his tongue and started at her in disgust.

Tears rolled down Tori's face as she stood there, still paralyzed. There was nothing she could say. The lifestyle that she'd tried to bury in the dark had been brought to the light. She felt her legs again, and she just turned and walked away. There were no goodbyes. No hugs. No kisses. But Bo and Tori knew that they would never see each other again.

"Let's get the fuck outta here." Bo was angrier than his friends had ever seen him. They both thought he deserved to be mad. He'd thought Tori was the girl of his dreams. Dap and Tat followed his lead without saying a word.

Dap's mind was in overdrive, just like his friends' brains were. His thoughts went back to the night of the party, and he began asking some commonsense questions. "Tat, lemme ask you something. Did you use a condom that whole night?"

"Hell, yeah. I went through like three of them. I didn't have any on when they gave me head though. And I ain't gave none of them head."

"Okay, good." Dap thought that all was well since Bo hadn't had sex with Tori. Or had he?

"You never hit that huh, Bo?" Dap and Tat looked at their friend, not expecting the answer they were about to get.

"Yeah, I did. Just once. I smashed that day she came to my dorm when you were there. And I didn't even use a condom." By voicing his mistake, he suddenly felt like the biggest idiot in the world.

"Everything gon' be okay, Bo. You gon' bounce back from that. You're all over the TV and shit now. We gon get our results back negative, and we gon' take it from there. We won't let anything hold us down." Dap was trying to cheer his buddy up, but it clearly was not working.

The three friends were quiet for a while before Tat finally interrupted the silence. "Ay, Bo. You gotta admit it. That girl got some fiya ass…"

"SHUT UP, TAT!" Dap and Bo yelled simultaneously. They didn't even let Tat finish his ill-timed comment.

The trio decided to shoot pool at Geno's in hopes of forgetting about Bo's recent disappointment.

CHAPTER 17

W ith the biggest game of the season coming up in just a few days, Bo had just experienced an ugly break-up with Tori. The only girl he had paid attention to at LSU had turned out to be someone unworthy of his heart. He was the kind of guy who respected everyone, but every bit of respect that he had for Tori was gone now.

It's been three days since the boys got tested, and they are expecting the results now. At first, Dap was a nervous wreck. Bo had tried everything to keep him calm and optimistic. But then the tables had turned with the break-up. No matter what though, they were determined to get through it together.

Bo decided to spend the night by his parents' in an effort to acquire some peace and comfort for a little while before returning to campus and preparing for the SEC title game.

His favorite music is neo-soul, but here he lay in his bed, Lil Boosie blasting from his stereo speakers. "Big money! I like it! I used to have hoes…who triflin'! Now I got hoes…who dykin'! And it's exciting!"

Suddenly, his bedroom door burst open. "HAVE YOU LOST YOUR RABBIT ASS MIND? DON'T YOU DARE PLAY THAT SHIT IN MY HOUSE! TURN IT OFF! NOW!" Mrs. Johnson was rarely angry like this. But when Bo had told her what happened with Tori, she definitely wasn't going to let him become disrespectful or depressed because of it. No way. Not on her watch.

"Lebeau, you cannot sit around here and be down on yourself. I know you're used to things being fairly easy, but life can be really difficult at times. Do you think your father and I always had it this good? I worked in damn near every fast food restaurant in Baton Rouge before I got into the medical field. And your daddy was a player when I met him. I had to deal with all kinda bullshit before he got it together. But we loved each other and we fought to make it work. Now I'm not saying that you have to fight for Tori, but I am telling you to fight for yourself. Don't let this obstacle defeat you, son." Mrs.

Johnson could always make him smile if nobody else could.

"Thanks, ma." Just as Bo was giving his mother a hug, the doorbell rang. "I'll get it." As Bo exited his room, he brushed shoulders with his dad, who was standing in the hallway.

"Ay, I'm still a playa," Mr. Johnson said jokingly. He and Bo laughed. Mrs. Johnson entered the hallway and gave her husband a serious stare. He glanced at Bo before walking toward his bedroom.

"Man, mama wears the pants in this house!" Bo laughed loudly, teasing his father as he went to see who was at the front door. It was Dap. He had been expecting a phone call from the clinic all day, but he hadn't heard anything yet and was more nervous than ever.

"You heard anything yet? The lady said that the results would be in today. They close at five and it's four now. Something's wrong, man; I can feel it." Dap took a seat on the top step and looked at his phone, shaking his head.

"Chill out, bruh. She didn't say the results would be in today for sure. She said they could be in as early as today, but we might not even hear anything until next week." Bo closed the door and sat on the step next to Dap.

Dap's phone rang. They immediately looked at each other.

After pausing for a few seconds, Dap finally answered his phone.

His heart was pounding.

"Hello?" His voice was actually trembling.

"Hello? I'm calling for Daron Singleton." This was the call he'd been waiting for.

"Yes, ma'am. This is Daron." His heart went from beating twice as fast as it should be to not beating at all. He stopped breathing.

"Hi, Mr. Singleton. I'm calling in regard to your blood work. All of your tests came back negative. You have a clean bill of health, sir. If you have any questions or need assistance with any health issues, please feel free to call or come into our office." These words were music to Dap's ears. He sighed in relief, and his heart began to beat again.

"Thank you so much, ma'am!" If that lady was anywhere near him, he would have picked her up and given her the biggest hug she had ever gotten in her life.

"Sounds like good news. I told you everything would be alright. Dap, you have a fresh start. You're in college. You have a good woman, and I know you have money," he laughed a little at the surprised look Dap gave him. "Oh, you thought I forgot about how you threw fifteen grand at me like it was fifteen dollars? Look, God is giving you a chance to take advantage of a good situation. You can take something that wasn't so good and make it a beautiful thing. Do the right thing, man." Bo was extremely happy that his friend would be okay.

Another ring interrupted their conversation. This time it was Bo's phone. They gave each other that look again.

"Hello?" he answered cautiously.

"Hello? I'm calling for Lebeau Johnson." It was the same lady from the clinic who called Dap.

"Yes, ma'am. This is Lebeau." Bo looked at Dap and nodded, confirming that it was his turn to receive some news.

"Mr. Johnson, we'd like you to come in so we can discuss the results of your tests…" She was about to say something else before Bo questioned her.

"Hold up. How come you can't just tell me the results now?" Bo became slightly angry, but as the seconds ticked by he realized what it meant.

"I'm sorry, sir. We can't disclose this information over the phone. When can you…"

Bo no longer had enough strength in his hand to hold the phone. Free from his clutch, the phone fell onto the steps and tumbled all the way to the ground. His eyes became filled with tears, but none fell. He had no words. Bo just sat on the steps looking and feeling helpless.

Dap knew what all of this had to mean. But how could this be? Bo didn't deserve this. He wasn't some junkie who used needles. He didn't sleep with different women for fun and games. Why was this happening to him?

Suddenly, Bo hopped up and headed to his car. He didn't say a word. He didn't even pick his phone up from the ground.

Dap was left sitting alone on the steps. He watched his best friend jump into his Mercedes and pull off. He couldn't hold it in any longer. With his heart heavy and his eyes full, he began to sob like a kid who was being scolded.

"FUCK!" He cursed loud enough for everybody on the block to hear him. Face wet, he cried and cried.

The loud outburst was enough to gain the attention of Mr. and Mrs. Johnson. The front door opened.

"Is everything okay, Daron?" Mrs. Johnson saw that Dap had been crying, but she also noticed that neither her son nor his car was outside.

"Where's Lebeau?" She tried to remain calm as she watched Dap cry his heart out on their front steps.

"I'm sorry, Mrs. Johnson. I gotta go." He gathered enough strength in his legs to stand up and walk to his car. He drove off, leaving Mrs. Johnson's questions unanswered.

Mr. Johnson spotted Bo's phone on the ground. He walked down the steps and picked up the phone. The screen was cracked, but not enough to impede operation. He navigated through the menu until he found what he was looking for. He selected "recent calls" and noticed that Bo had just received a call. Mr. Johnson glanced at his wife, and then his eyes focused on the phone again. Although he had no clue what to expect, he dialed out to that last incoming number.

CHAPTER 18

Bo had been driving and crying for hours. With no destination in mind, he merged onto Interstate 10 and headed west. He was entering Houston when he realized that he was low on gas.

He stopped at a gas station to use the restroom and fill his tank. While pumping his gas, he thought about purchasing a cheap phone just to call his parents and let them know he was okay.

Instead, he decided to book a hotel room for a couple of days and stay to himself. He wasn't ready to deal with all the questions and the attention. He just wanted to be alone for a while.

After deciding on a hotel and paying for a room, Bo ordered room service. He ate and watched SportsCenter. His mind was clear for a moment, but it didn't take long for the focus to be on the LSU Tigers. Bo's eyes were glued to the television as the sports analyst talked about his emergence as a starter on one of the top defenses in the nation.

He began to ask himself questions. How would he tell his coaches and teammates? How would the general public perceive him? How long would he live? Had Tori been tested? Would his parents be disappointed? The tears began to form once again.

Finally, Bo stretched across the comfortable king-sized bed and cried himself to sleep.

Bo's parents sat on the front steps of their home comforting each other. It had been years since the last time they had sat outside this late. They'd been worrying about their son since he drove off earlier without his phone. Mr. Johnson held his wife tight and tried his best to convince her that everything would be okay.

Suddenly a car pulled up in front of their residence. It was Dap. He got out of his Cadillac and walked slowly toward the couple.

"Hey, I was just stopping by to see if Bo came back or if y'all…"

Before Dap could finish his statement, a cop car pulled up behind his car. They all began to question themselves about whether the officer had bad news about Bo or if he was there for Dap. The cop got out of his car and made his way into the Johnson's yard. Mr. and Mrs. Johnson stood up and greeted the gentlemen.

"Hi, officer. What can we do for you?" Bo's father spoke as the officer approached.

The officer didn't answer. He simply stopped just a few yards away from the group and watched them. He glanced at the Johnsons for a few seconds before turning his attention to Dap. Mr. and Mrs. Johnson looked at each other, confused.

"Is there a problem?" Dap spoke in an aggressive, irritated tone. He didn't appreciate the fact that the cop had ignored Mr. Johnson. With an evil grin on his face, the cop removed his cap. He stared into Dap's eyes and waited for movement. Dap's heart skipped a few beats

He didn't even give Dap a chance. The glock 45 slid from its holster with quickness and ease. Two bullets ripped through Dap's chest. Mrs. Johnson began to scream as her husband grabbed her to escape the unexpected danger. Tiko then fired a shot into Mr.

Johnson's back, causing the man to fall on top of his wife. Mrs.

Johnson cried and screamed as she fought to remove herself from her husband's weight, but she had nowhere to go. Tiko was already upon her.

She just stopped screaming, stopped cold. If she was gonna die today, she might as well be brave about it. "I don't know who you are or why you're doing this, but my God in heaven is watching you, and you will get what you deserve." She closed her eyes and began to pray."

"You see. That's where you're wrong, lady. I already too my lick, and thanks to Dap, you're about to take yours." Tiko squatted down and placed the barrel of the gun against the back of Mrs. Johnson's head. Then there was a loud blast."

"Nooooooooooooo!" Bo yelled loudly as he popped up from his disturbed sleep. He had been having the worst nightmare imaginable. He fought to catch his breath, but it wasn't easy. His heart seemed to be beating at twice its normal rate, and he was sweating like an escaped inmate with K-9s on his tail.

"What the hell was that? Damn this. I need to go home." Bo quickly put on his clothes and grabbed his keys. In only a few minutes, he was back on I-10 and on his way home to Baton Rouge.

CHAPTER 19

The sun rose slowly above the horizon, exposing a beautiful clear sky. This was indeed a gorgeous morning. With the last twenty-four hours of his life being so hectic, so out of control, Bo was thankful to at least see such a beautiful day. He wondered how many more of them he had left.

He pulled into his parents' driveway and sat in his car. He had already turned the music down really low in an effort not to wake his parents. Flashbacks of his vivid nightmare zipped through his mind as he gazed at the front steps.

Just as the tears began to form in his eyes, the front door opened and snapped him out of his trance. Mrs. Johnson smiled, happier than ever to see her one and only son. Bo smiled back at his mother. He got out of the car, crossed the yard, and walked up the steps to give his mother the longest hug she had ever received from her baby boy.

"I love you so much, mama. I don't even care what I have to go through. I'm not even worried about what people are gonna say. All that matters to me is the ones I love. As long as I have y'all, I'mma be okay."

Bo finally pried himself away from his mother and saw his father standing right behind her.

"Pops, I never forgot the lesson you taught me. You always told me that there's one thing about life to remember. I have to play that hand that I'm dealt. And I'm gonna play it with my head held high. I'mma play to win. I won't lay down. I won't give up. My life isn't over; it's just beginning." Bo gave his dad a hug and told him that he loved him.

"That's my boy. Words can't describe how much I love you and how proud I am of you. You want some breakfast?" Mr.

Johnson didn't even wait for an answer. He simply led the way into the kitchen.

"I'm starving. I guess y'all knew I was too worked up to eat. My stomach been growling since…who are you?"

The young lady sitting at the kitchen table caught Bo totally off guard. He had never seen her before. What was she doing in his parents' kitchen at seven o'clock in the morning?

It was obvious that she had been crying. Her eyes were red and watery. "Hi, Lebeau. You don't know me. I'm the one who called about your results. My name is Taylor. You don't have HIV. Your parents called the clinic after you…"

"What? Hold up. Wait. Wait. Wait." Bo didn't know if he should be relieved or angry. He looked at his parents and they were smiling. Bow as extremely confused.

"Somebody please tell me what is going on." Bo was obviously frustrated.

Please forgive me. Everything is my fault. See, I'm a HUGE LSU fan, and I'm probably your biggest fan. I recognized your name, and I just was trying to get you to come in so I could see you up close and personal. I wanted you to see me, so I could tell you that I'm your biggest fan. You don't have any STDs." Taylor felt embarrassed and ashamed after putting Bo and his family through so much trouble.

Mr. Johnson filled in the rest of the puzzle pieces. "I picked up your phone and saw their number. It was the last incoming call. That's how we were able to piece everything together. Nice story

to tell the grandkids, hunh?" Mr. Johnson was trying to put a smile on his son's face, but it was clearly not working at the moment.

"Again. I'm sorry. I'm so sorry. I guess I should be going." Taylor grabbed her purse and headed toward the door.

"Hold up." Bo caught up with her. "Look, we all make mistakes, right? I mean you still gave me some good news this morning. And I got to meet my biggest fan." Finally, a smile appeared on his face. He hugged Taylor and walked her outside.

"Look at our son. I think we did a fine job raising that boy. What do you think is going to happen now?" Mrs. Johnson walked over to her husband. She had stayed up all night praying for God to bring her child back to her. Her prayers had been answered.

Mr. Johnson put his arm around his wife and whispered in her ear. "He's gonna play the hand he's been dealt."

They walked to the front door and took a glance outside. They watched their son holding his biggest fan in his arms. No words. He just held her. He was simply playing the hand he had been dealt.

EPILOGUE

———

Dap was never one to stay in bed late on a Sunday morning. It's routine for him to get up before 8 a.m. and say his prayers before cooking breakfast. But today was much different from any other Sunday. He made a promise to Tamara that he made sure not to break.

"So....what's the name of this church again?" Dap tried his best not to make his nervousness obvious.

"True Light Worship Center." Tamara glanced at Dap. He hadn't said much so far.

"Are you okay? I know this is different for you, but you are gonna enjoy the service."

"I'm fine." The guilt of lying while on his way to church hit Dap instantly.

Okay, I'm not fine. I'm nervous. I'm super nervous. It's been years since I've been inside of a church."

Tamara placed her hand on Dap's leg. "I admire you for keeping your promise and coming to church with me. It really means a lot to me."

A slight grin appeared on Dap's face. "I must be getting some tonight, huh?"

He laughed out loud as he prepared himself for the response that he knew was coming. "Boy!!!"

Tamara spanked his leg as she laughed.

"This is it coming up. Turn here."

Dap felt his heart pounding as though it was trying to escape from behind his rib cage. He found a parking space and the couple made their way to the church's front entrance. The double doors opened just as they reached them.

"Good morning!! " an elderly woman cheerfully greeted them as they entered.

"Good morning". They returned the gesture. Then usher guided them to their seats.

"Is everybody happy like this every Sunday?" Dap didn't remember people being this happy when he went to church as a young boy. Everybody was really serious. Just as they were sitting, the preacher's voice roared through the speakers.

"This is the day that the Lord has made. Let us rejoice!!!!" Pastor Claiborne began to speak on how he used to run the streets, getting into fights and getting drunk all the time. This caught Dap off guard but he could relate to it so well. All kinds of thoughts entered Dap's mind as Pastor Claiborne handed the program over to the choir. Chills traveled through Dap as he listened. Tears begin to roll down his face. So much has gone on in his life. He had already made changes, but he knew that more changes needed to be made. Tamara put an arm around him, comforting him as she sang along with the choir. There were shouts of praise from all over the church. Pastor's sermon was about second chances and forgiveness. He spoke about how God loves us so much that He gives us chance after chance to get our acts together. He also mentioned that we have no one to blame if we fail to listen to God. As the sermon came to a close, Pastor asked if there was anyone who hadn't accepted Christ in their life. He spoke on how tomorrow isn't promised. A teenage boy walked toward Pastor and everybody clapped and shouted with excitement. Then a middle aged man went. Then a little girl. Dap leaned over and whispered in Tamara's ear.

"Thank you so much. I think you have saved my life." He kissed her on the cheek and cried before he made his way down the aisle.

"Give God glory, people! Come on, brother!! Praise God!!" Pastor noticed the pain and hurt in Dap. He stepped down and went to meet him. "Young man, I've never seen you before in my life. But I want you to know that it was meant for you to be here today. And I want you to know that God loves you and He has a special purpose for your life."

Before Dap got a chance to speak, he was on the receiving end of a big hug. Tamara was behind him with her arms around him, squeezing him tightly. She cried like never before. She just rested her head on his back, held him tight, and cried her eyes out.

"Look at this, church. Isn't this beautiful? This is a blessing. Angels are in heaven rejoicing over this. God is so good. He is worthy!!" Even Pastor Claiborne was in tears as members of the congregation walked toward the front of the church. Everybody was shouting and giving praise to God, shaking hands and hugging one another.

With his face wet from his tears and Tamara still clinging to him, Dap looked up toward heaven.

"God, thank you for saving my life. Thank you for another chance."